Micky the Mighty Magpie

For Buba and Zaida, loving and loved. J.F.
For Philip. M.W.

Viking Kestrel
Penguin Books Australia Ltd,
487 Maroondah Highway, P.O. Box 257 Ringwood, Victoria, 3134, Australia
Penguin Books Ltd, Harmondsworth, Middlesex, England
Viking Penguin Inc., 40 West 23rd Street, New York, N.Y. 10010, U.S.A.
Penguin Books Canada Ltd, 2801 John Street, Markham, Ontario, Canada, L3R 1B4
Penguin Books (N.Z.) Ltd, 182-190 Wairau Road, Auckland 10, New Zealand

First published 1986 by Viking

Copyright © June Factor, 1986
Illustrations copyright © Melissa Webb, 1986

Typeset in Palatino by Dovatype, Melbourne

Made and printed in Singapore by
Tien Wah Press

Factor, June.
Micky the mighty magpie.

ISBN 0 670 80788 5.

1. Children's stories, Australian. I. Webb,
Melissa, 1960-   . II. Title.

A823'.3

MICKY

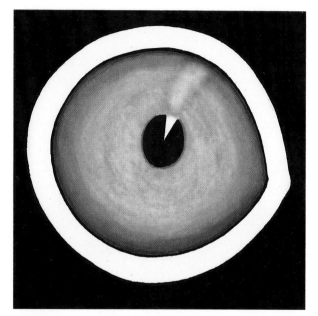

THE MIGHTY
MAGPIE

by June Factor illustrated by Melissa Webb

VIKING KESTREL

Micky is the largest magpie in the world.

He is gigantic.

He is enormous.

Well, he is very big — for a magpie.

He lives in the wattle tree in our backyard.

What makes Micky such a remarkable magpie is not just his size.

He also has some very remarkable habits.

He enjoys eating cheese.

He likes his bird bath to be lukewarm.

And he picks holes in rubber hoses.

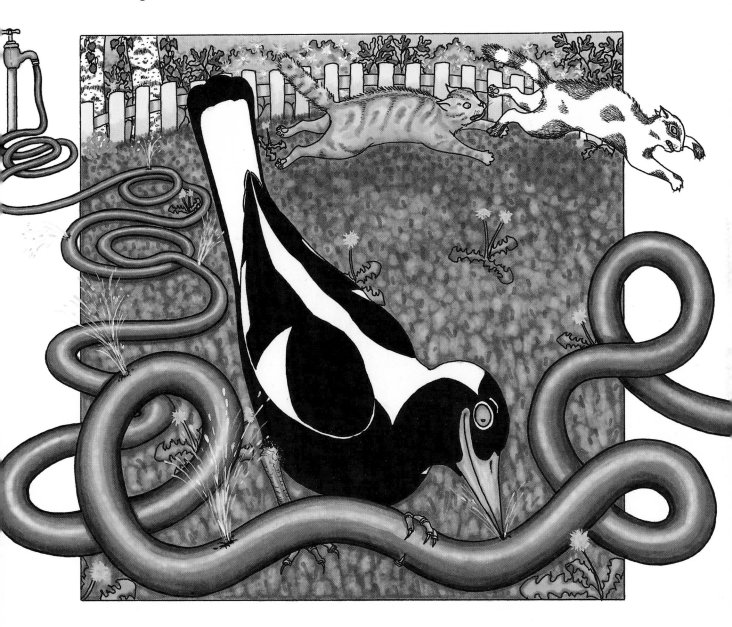

That, of course, is not just a habit.
It's a bad habit.
Almost a crime.

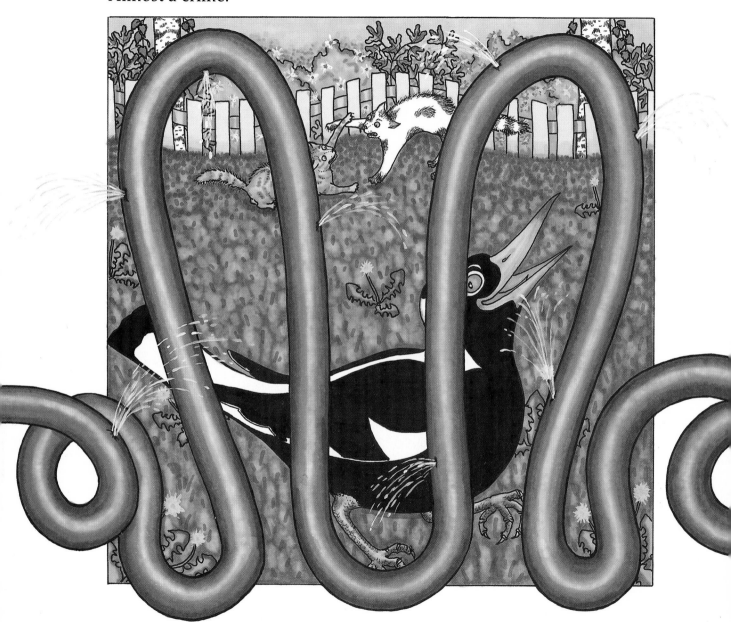

It could turn the hose into a long, skinny shower.

Naturally, I tried to cure him of this bad habit.
I scolded him when I saw him pick, pick, picking.

I offered him delicious tit-bits.

He preferred the hose.

Naomi, who is twelve, and very wise, said:
'Why don't we put away the hose?
Then he won't be tempted.'

An excellent idea — except that we need that hose.
How else could we water the garden?

How else could we wash the car?

And what if the house caught fire?
What is the use of a hose coiled up
in the shed at a time like that?

Ian, who is ten, and very clever, said:
'We should examine his brain.
It might have something missing.'

Well, and what if Micky's brain
should also turn out to be remarkable?
Would that stop him ruining the hose?

Sylvia, who is eight, and very smart, said:
'You'll make him nervous, and then
he won't sing anymore.'

Oh. That could be serious.
Micky is the mightiest singer, the greatest, the finest . . .
well, he is very good at warbling and trilling.

You can't interfere with the great musicians
of the world, even if they do have odd habits.

So Micky is allowed to go on picking at the hose.
Now water comes out of sixteen holes,
not just the one at the end.

Which is really very good for the garden.

And we can use a bucket to wash the car.

And nobody plays with matches in this house,
so we're not likely to get burnt down.

There's no doubt about it — Micky is a mighty magpie!

The Author

Born in Poland, June Factor came to Australia as an infant. She has been a teacher, scriptwriter, children's radio producer, book reviewer, and is well-known as a children's folklorist. She lectures in English and Children's Literature at the Institute of Early Childhood Development in Melbourne.

She has three children and two cats, and many birds live in her old, scraggly but pleasant garden. Her previous books include *Far Out, Brussel Sprout!, Big Dipper, Big Dipper Rides Again* and *A First Australian Poetry Book.*

Born in Melbourne, Victoria, Melissa Webb is a self-taught artist. At the age of nineteen she ran an extremely quiet antique shop, where she had plenty of time to draw, and at night played synthesizer in a band.

She now works as a freelance illustrator, part-time jewellery maker and cat trainer. She has four cats (one of them appears in this book), and a raucous and rather vulgar budgerigar.

Melissa's Ambition is to achieve something worth putting in her biography.

The Illustrator